Rhyme Time TOWN
LET'S HELP HUMPTY!

Adapted by Patty Michaels

Ready-to-Read

Simon Spotlight
New York London Toronto Sydney New Delhi

SIMON SPOTLIGHT
An imprint of Simon & Schuster Children's Publishing Division
1230 Avenue of the Americas, New York, New York 10020
This Simon Spotlight edition December 2020
DreamWorks Rhyme Time Town © 2020 DreamWorks Animation LLC.
All Rights Reserved.
Manufactured in the United States of America 1020 LAK
10 9 8 7 6 5 4 3 2 1
ISBN 978-1-5344-7977-7 (hc)
ISBN 978-1-5344-7976-0 (pbk)
ISBN 978-1-5344-7978-4 (eBook)

Daisy and Cole
are playing.

They are pretending
to be knights.

Humpty Dumpty

wants to play too.

His mom, Mumpty, wants him to be careful. "Remember what happened last time?" she says.

"Humpty Dumpty sat on a wall. Humpty Dumpty had a great fall," Daisy and Cole say.

"No walls, no falls.
To be safe and sound,
stay on the ground,"
Mumpty says.

Daisy, Cole, and Humpty
head to the woods.

Humpty climbs a tree.

Daisy and Cole

climb the tree too.

Oh no!

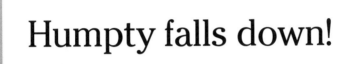

Humpty falls down!

His shell is cracked.

Daisy and Cole cannot
put his shell
back together again.

They ask Jack and Jill
for help.

They all put Humpty

back together again!

But Humpty is afraid
to keep playing.

He does not want to
break his shell again.

Daisy and Cole
will make armor
to protect his shell.

Jack and Jill

will help.

They will test the armor
on a watermelon.

If the watermelon
does not crack,
Humpty will not either.

Daisy and Cole

make wooden armor.

The watermelon breaks!

Then they tie balloons around the watermelon. That does not work either.

Then they use
a feather pillow
to make puffy armor.

It works!

Humpty now has armor
made out of
pillow feathers!

"Now we can keep playing," Daisy says. "Hooray!"